PETER RABBIT 2™

LITTLE RABBIT, BIG CITY!

F. WARNE & CO.

MEET THE CHARACTERS

Bunnies have been hopping around in the McGregors' garden ever since anyone can remember. And no wonder – the enormous vegetable patch is a sight to see! Its walls are lined with row after row of ripe radishes, budding beanstalks, and leafy lettuces.

Sadly, ever since anyone can remember, the bunnies have been banned from putting a paw on the McGregors' veggies. If Peter Rabbit and his family wanted to crunch on a carrot, they had to creep into the garden and steal one . . .

. . . until Thomas McGregor fell in love with Peter's friend, Bea.

Bea adored animals, especially the little fluffy bunnies that hopped around her home. She painted pictures of Peter Rabbit, and made sure that he was well looked after.

When Peter watched Thomas and Bea get married, he was happy.
They all became one big happy family.

Peter wasn't the only bunny Bea loved. There was also his cousin Benjamin and his sisters Flopsy, Mopsy, and Cotton-tail.

But Bea had a dream for Peter. She hoped that Thomas could be a new dad for her best bunny! Peter's real father wasn't around anymore – he had gone to the great pie in the sky.

After Thomas and Bea's wedding, the rabbits were allowed to visit the vegetable patch whenever they liked.

Only one area stayed out-of-bounds. Thomas's tomato garden was a creature-free zone. There were no exceptions. When it came to growing tomatoes, Thomas McGregor was very particular.

Everybody knew the rules, but those tomatoes looked so good! Even Bea struggled not to steal a bite every now and then.

One day, when Bea was painting Peter's portrait, Thomas rushed into the house. "I think they are ready," he said, holding up his finest specimens.

Thomas had decided to take his tomatoes to the city. He wanted to sell his harvest at the farmer's market.

Peter went outside to eat his supper. He hopped into the vegetable patch, just in time to see old Tommy Brock rustling around in the tomato garden.

The old badger reached up and grabbed the reddest, juiciest tomato on the plot. "NO!" shouted Peter, ordering him to hand it over. "Those are Mr. McGregor's!"

Tommy had known Peter since he was a twinkle in his dad's eye. Animals had always been stealing from the McGregors. "Because he married the lady, you do what he says now?"

Peter twitched his nose. "Just don't touch the tomatoes."

Peter was trying to tidy everything up when he heard a knocking noise. Thomas had seen him through a window!

"Leave my tomatoes alone!" bellowed Thomas.

"It wasn't me," sighed Peter, holding up his paws. The stolen tomato dropped onto the ground. "Uh-oh."

It can be hard to be a rabbit. Now Peter was in trouble again and it wasn't even his fault. He missed his dad more than ever.

The next time Thomas went into the city, Peter stowed himself away in the back of his truck. He needed to get away from it all. In the city, Peter would be free to be himself. He could make a new start.

It didn't take long to find some new friends. Peter couldn't believe it when he bumped into an old rabbit who had been pals with his pop! Barnabas decided that Peter was "a fierce, bad rabbit, just like him."

Barnabas introduced Peter to the rest of his crew:
Tom Kitten, Samuel Whiskers, and Mittens.
None of them were scared to eat a silly tomato.
They stole food out of swanky restaurants!

Now Peter could take whatever he wanted,
and there was no one there to tell him off.

But Peter wasn't really a fierce, bad rabbit.
He started to miss Bea and the garden.

Barnabas couldn't care less. He persuaded Peter to do a job with him. It was a big job. The old crook didn't really remember the bunny's dad. He lied so Peter would help him raid the farmer's market with the other animals!

Peter felt alone . . . until a familiar face appeared. Thomas had come to save him!

"It's what dads do," he said.

It was good to be home again. Thomas was still fussy about his tomatoes, but Peter didn't mind.

Families – it turns out – came in all shapes and sizes.